STAR WARS™

EGMONT
We bring stories to life

First published in Great Britain 2015
by Egmont UK Limited, The Yellow Building,
1 Nicholas Road, London W11 4AN

Written by Katrina Pallant
Designed by Maddox Philpot

© & ™ 2015 Lucasfilm Ltd.

ISBN 978 1 4052 8047 1
62521/1
Printed in Italy

For more great *Star Wars* books, visit www.egmont.co.uk/starwars

Stay safe online. Any website addresses listed in this book are correct at the time of going to print. However, Egmont is not responsible for content hosted by third parties. Please be aware that online content can be subject to change and websites can contain content that is unsuitable for children. We advise that all children are supervised when using the internet.

Rey makes her living scavenging through crashed starships looking for items she can sell. Delete every second letter to discover where Rey lives.

START

S K B U T P K L N A F N I E Y T O J P D Q K S ?

General Leia Organa sends her best X-wing pilot, Poe Dameron, on a very important mission. Copy the colours to bring this resistance fighter to life.

Poe arrives on Jakku with his trusty droid, BB-8.
Draw this spherical, loyal astromech using the grid as a guide.

Poe meets with Leia's old friend to receive a map to the location of Luke Skywalker. Replace each letter with the one before it in the alphabet to reveal the name of this trusted ally.

MPS TBO UFLLB

The First Order invades Jakku and the stormtroopers attack the villagers. But one trooper is not like his fellow soldiers and only pretends to shoot his blaster. Can you find trooper FN-2187 below?

A

B

C

D

E

F

Hint: he is not like the others.

Kylo Ren captures Poe and interrogates him to find out the location of the map. Find five differences between these two pictures of the menacing villain.

FN-2187's actions are investigated by his commanding officer. She is different from other troopers, with her reflective armour. Complete the sequences to find out this captain's name.

1. B, P, B, P, B, P, B, ____

2. H, H, A, H, H, A, H, ____

3. P, A, L, P, A, L, P, ____

4. R, E, R, S, R, E, R, ____

5. L, M, M, L, M, M, L, ____

6. Q, Q, R, A, Q, Q, R, ____

Poe hid the map with BB-8 before he was captured and instructed the droid to run away. Follow the tangled lines to discover who finds BB-8.

A

B

C

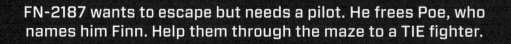

FN-2187 wants to escape but needs a pilot. He frees Poe, who names him Finn. Help them through the maze to a TIE fighter.

START

FINISH

© LFL

STICKER SCENES

The stormtroopers are on patrol, but one trooper has turned up with the wrong helmet. Can you find the flametrooper amongst the stormtroopers?

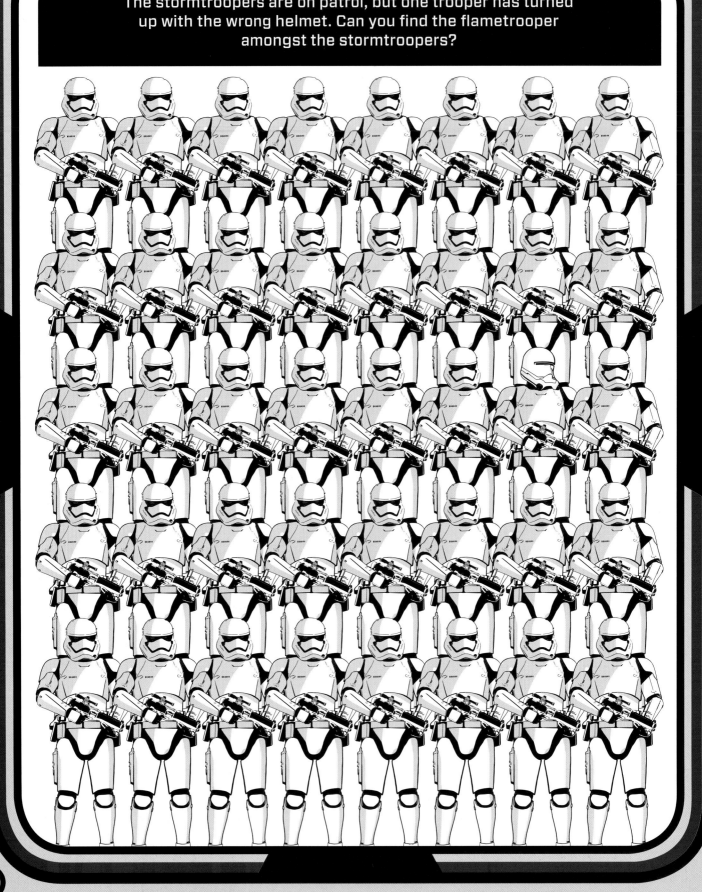

After Finn and Poe are separated, Finn teams up
with Rey to escape the stormtroopers on Jakku.
Find the right pieces to complete this action scene.

Rey and Finn are being shot at by TIE fighters and must find their way to a vehicle to escape. Answer the sums and follow the correct answers to find out which one they steal.

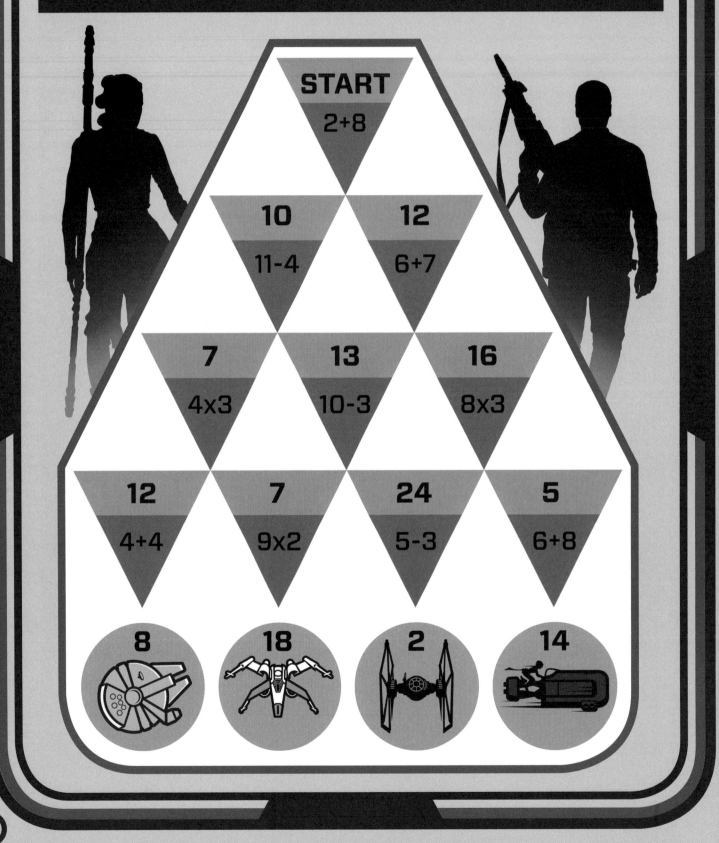

START
2+8

10
11-4

12
6+7

7
4x3

13
10-3

16
8x3

12
4+4

7
9x2

24
5-3

5
6+8

8

18

2

14

To escape the TIE fighters pursuing the *Millennium Falcon* Rey flies it through a Super Star Destroyer. Help her through the wreckage by following the pattern through the maze, moving up, down, left and right.

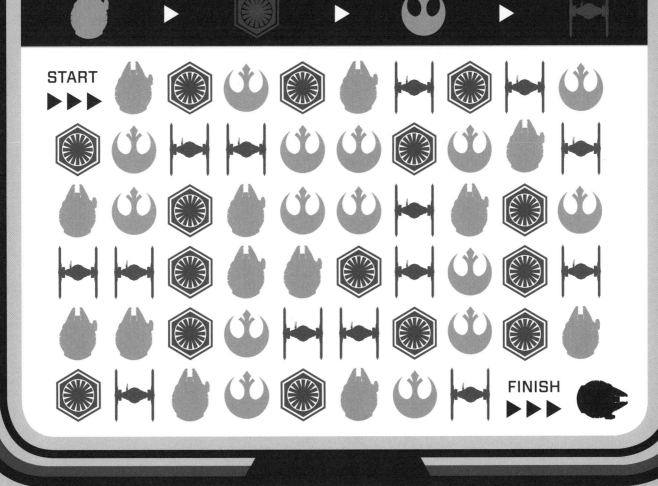

START
▶▶▶

FINISH
▶▶▶

The *Millennium Falcon* is pulled into another ship's cargo bay, and its former owners, Han and Chewbacca, board. Which of the below images of the Wookiee matches the big one exactly?

A

B

E

D

C

A powerful army known as the First Order threatens to conquer the free worlds. Complete the grid putting one, and only one, of each image in every row, column and 2x3 box.

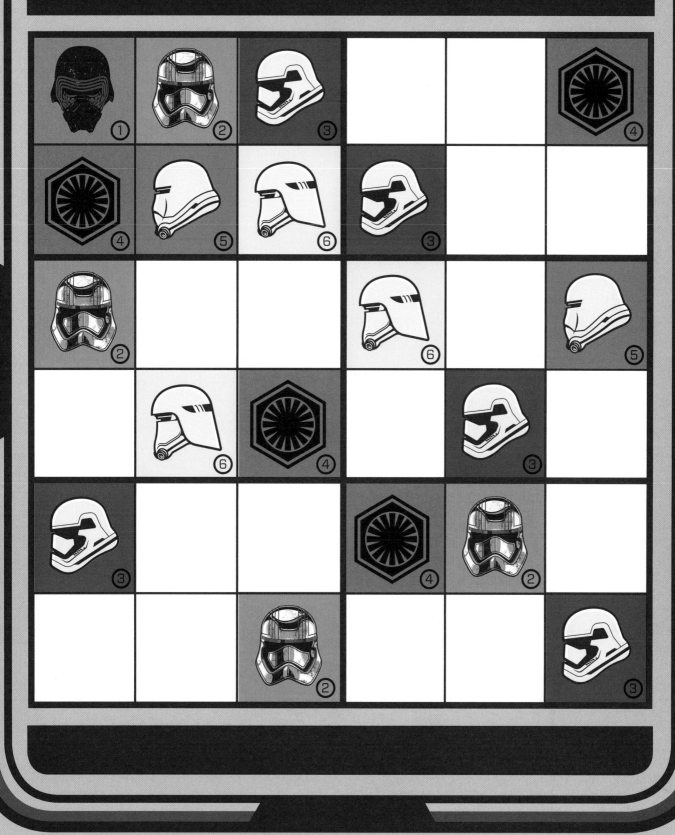

The Force Awakens introduces you to many new characters as well as bringing back some old favourites. Find as many as you can in this wordsearch.

B	R	E	Y	S	H	A	L	V	R	O	E	V	V	E
E	O	P	A	J	D	A	L	A	J	I	Z	H	K	Z
R	B	R	D	D	N	Q	M	Y	E	P	X	U	V	K
H	C	E	E	L	U	S	A	T	K	E	L	X	J	Y
O	D	T	K	B	A	P	W	Z	U	E	A	C	U	L
T	P	T	G	H	W	T	H	R	N	R	E	H	G	O
L	T	W	P	C	S	T	V	Y	V	H	C	E	X	R
E	O	U	N	N	I	F	Y	O	Z	T	W	W	J	E
P	O	R	L	J	E	G	B	Y	U	V	C	B	X	N
R	E	O	S	P	N	E	Z	A	V	E	Z	A	D	I
G	U	A	V	A	R	E	M	M	I	Q	A	C	S	I
P	H	N	Z	D	N	A	A	A	O	B	I	C	U	B
K	Q	F	A	Y	V	T	K	I	I	R	E	A	X	W
S	W	N	J	Q	I	Q	E	N	S	U	L	G	W	K
Z	D	G	P	G	H	M	W	K	U	A	R	T	O	O
N	I	X	X	A	O	A	W	E	K	Q	K	Z	H	B
U	D	D	N	S	M	D	B	U	C	A	E	R	R	M

Rey   Phasma
Finn   Peazy
Kylo Ren   Poe
Hux   Zuvio
Han   Sarco
Leia   Vober Dand
Chewbacca   Tasu Leech
Artoo   Lor San Tekka
Threepio   Unkar Plutt
Luke

PAGE 2: **Planet Jakku**

PAGE 4: **Lor San Tekka**

PAGE 6: **D**

PAGE 7:

PAGE 8: **PHASMA**

PAGE 9: **Path A (Rey)**

PAGE 10:

PAGE 20:

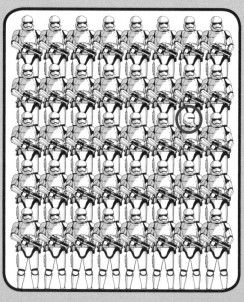

PAGE 21: **1 - D, 2 - C, 3 - E, 4 - F, 5 - G**

PAGE 22:

PAGE 23:

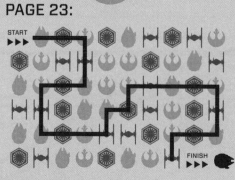

PAGE 24: **D**

PAGE 27:

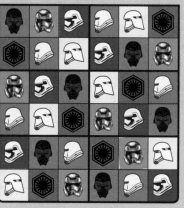

PAGE 28:

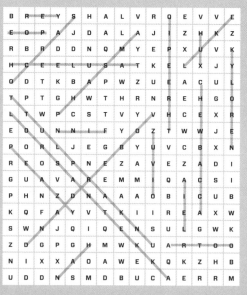